100(ISH) 100-WORD STORIES

100(ish) delectable and delightful
100-word stories written by
Ian and Glad for Colne Radio's
Bill's Big Bag of Onions.

Ian Hornett and
Gladys Hornett

CONTENTS

100 (ish)
100-Word Stories

ISBN: 9798865910794

ABOUT THIS BOOK

This book is a compilation of over one-hundred 100-word stories, written by me, Ian Hornett, and my mum, Gladys Hornett.

There are 114 stories in total, not quite enough for one a day but certainly enough for one every 3.20175439 days.

What is the book about?

Well, what better way to explain than by using the 100-word format which is the basis in which the stories are written?

On the next page you will find – in exactly 100 words – the what, the why, the who, the where and the when.

The What, The Why, The Who, The Where and The When (by Ian)

My mum and I have been writing 100-word stories for a radio show on **Colne Radio** called **Bill's Big Bag of Onions** – officially described as:

'Radio journeys through seductive soundscapes of cool and beguiling music, blended with unique and original 100-word short stories, written exclusively for the show by our listeners and voiced by our team of award-winning actors.'

What are Onions, I hear you ask? Why do you write them? Who is Bill? Where do you get your ideas from? When did you start writing Onions?
Since it's only 100 words, do you sometimes run out of words before

FAMILY

Banjo joy (Glad)

Christmas day was always just the family: mum, dad, children and grandmas, Christmas dinner, presents – always great fun.

But Boxing Day was the day the aunts and uncles came.

Mum and dad would prepare food, cold meats, pickles, cakes, sandwiches, sausage rolls. An uncle would go to the off-licence to buy beer for the men, a bottle of sherry for the ladies. Squash for the children! More presents from the relatives, then the evening fun. Songs around the piano, stories, games, the laughter getting louder as time wore on.

But for me, my dad plinking his banjo was the highlight.

Cantankerous (Glad)

Ivy arrived home, bags full of food for the party later that day. She opened the door to see Tom painting the bannisters.

'What are you doing? People will get paint all over their clothes!'

'You said it needed doing. They will just have to be careful!'

The day passed. Painting finished, food prepared, children ready. Bannisters still very tacky. Notices put up:

WET PAINT!

Just before the guests arrived, Ivy looked at Tom. 'You can't wear that jumper! It has holes in the elbows'.

Grumbling, Tom went upstairs. He reappeared in a different jumper... with holes in the elbows.

I have a Dream (Ian)

'I had a strange dream last night.'

Oh no – please don't tell me.

'I was in our house… but it wasn't our house.'

Course you were.

'Lesley was there. So were you, Mum and Gran, for some reason! How weird was that!'

Not weird. We live with you.

'Gran was eating an apple. Suddenly…'

It turned into a doughnut? A rabbit?

'It turned into a hedgehog.'

Close. Let me guess – then you flew around.

'Then I flew around! Unbelievable!'

Not really. It was a dream.

'So weird. D'you ever have dreams like that?'

No!

'What d'you think this is then?'

Grandma (Glad)

'Grandma's here!'

Hooray! Hugs and treats!

During her stay she would share my bed, and at night I would listen to her gentle snoring.

By day, Grandma and Mum would catch up on news from the family. For us, there were cuddles, or a wink and smile if our parents were cross with us.

But dinner time we enjoyed the most. Our eyes grew wide as Grandma carefully poured her Guinness, then, with trembling hand, raised the creamy foam liquid and took her first sip before smacking her lips.

To us, it looked the most delicious drink ever invented!

That's My Boy! (Ian)

He might be just married but he's still my little boy.

I'm in the bathroom about to have a shave this morning when I hear two requests through the door:

'Dad, can I borrow your trainers? I wanna go for a run and I've lost mine.' And then another, more urgent: 'Dad, can I have a quick pee in there before I go? I'm desperate.'

Rather reluctantly, I acquiesce.

10 minutes later I return to the bathroom to be met with the most obnoxious smell.

And if that wasn't bad enough... the culprit's sodding well run off with my shoes!

Sibling rivalry (Ian)

My twin thinks he's better than I am.

I hate the way he stares at me – scathing, critical, loathing. It hurts and I show it. I'm weak. He knows that. He mimics my pathetic face, then laughs. I try to laugh back, mimicking him. It has no effect. He comes back stronger, throwing daggers at me. I get angry, shout and scream. He just waits until I've finished before pulling that supercilious face that makes me feel so small.

I hate my twin. I should avoid him really but when I shave without a mirror, I cut myself to bits.

They Know Me There (Ian)

'They know me there,' my Nan used to boast after every appointment or shop visit.

Our responses? Bet they do! With flame-coloured hair, a physique and temperament built to withstand air raids, Ivy was unforgettable. She could laugh at herself though. Like the time she stopped at her dentists, hoping they could deal with a troublesome tooth. The man suggested a follow-up.

Grateful, she arrived a few days later to be told that it hadn't been a dentist for over 6 years.

'Wouldn't mind,' she recounted, 'but the cheeky beggar I'd seen spent 5 minutes looking inside my bleedin' mouth!'

What? (Ian)

Brother and sister for over 80 years they'd always been close. With poor hearing increasingly an issue, they were forced to get closer still. TV was a problem too. Even on full volume, it was muffled.

'Why don't you switch the wotsits on?'

'What?'

'The wotsits - you know, with words.'

'Oh, the thingamies.'

'Thingamies?'

'What are they called? The doodahs.'

'The what?'

'With words along the bottom?'

'Yes! Words.'

'What are they called?'

'Can't think,'

'This is ridiculous!'

'There's a button on the remote.'

'A what on where?'

If only they didn't just do subtitles on the telly.

HOME

The Outing (Glad)

Bob saw the poster on his way to work:

Free rail tickets and tea to see the new housing estate.

Recently married, living in rented rooms, weekends were spent relaxing: pictures, bus to Epping Forest, visit mums, walking round London.

They had always lived in the East End, close to family and work. Their sort didn't own their homes. But a quick look around, tea and back home would be fun.

However, when they saw the houses with front and back gardens... roads called Avenues or Drives, open spaces... smitten, they had to live there.

They did... for 60 years!

A Bad Case of Wind (Ian)

Another storm batters us and I'm on edge. Hyper-sensitive? Maybe. As a kid I had to read a book to class with the phrase, 'Woo-woo-woo, went the wind'. Sounded ridiculous, so embarrassing!

Newly moved into our house in 1987, a hurricane hit, and our shed roof flew into the police car park.

Ten years later, our poplars destroyed the neighbour's coy carp pond.

Now, with every gust, I get a feeling of trepidation. I should put my worries in a box, compartmentalise them. I need firmer boundaries!

Then perhaps, when the wind woo-woos, I wouldn't lose the bloody fence panels.

Home is Where the Heart Was (Ian)

There had been much discussion on the decor and soft furnishings.

Since he would be the one spending most the time inside staring at it, he had favoured something soothing, not too busy on the eye. His wife had favoured white, but he was less keen on light colours.

In the end, there had been a compromise: peach... and cushions all round, of course. It was comfortable and practical, he reflected, accessible, yet off the beaten track. A place he could come back to.

Home.

With that happy thought, he smiled, pushed open the lid and stepped out the coffin.

A New Shed on the Block (Ian)

The shed – rotten wood, ramshackle, condemned – creaked and groaned under the weight of its contents. There was a new shed on the block: solid metal, watertight... smart.

Out of the old, into the new went garden implements, power tools, paint pots, deckchairs, golf clubs, car accessories, petrol lawnmower, boxes.

Well, not quite all – a miscalculation. Solid metal, watertight, smart... but too small. Dark clouds loomed, and half a shed load still on the lawn.

Out of the new, back into the old.

The new shed on the block – now a lawnmower's garage. Not as smart as it thought it was.

Gutter Pain (Ian)

He leans out the window and watches water splurge over the side of the gutter, the house drowning in its own tears. Another blockage. More money down the drain. It's too high for him to fix that one.

In the garden, the shed is crying in sympathy.
Still, a much more accessible gutter, a stepladder job well within his DIY capabilities. It's forming quite the puddle, upset by neglect in recent times.

4 solid legs; 4 steps up, a failed adjustment; a wobble, a grab, 4 steps down... the hard way.

Cut, battered and bruised – more tears.

That's gutter hurt.

The Project Manager (Ian)

Eight contractors on site to complete the annex. Pressure's on to get the work done on time and to spec. I'm project managing – of course. I won't relinquish control at this crucial stage.

We meet, instructions are succinct – exactly what's needed, but like all good project managers, I listen carefully, playback what's been said. One mistake and... well, the consequences are dire. We part ways – clear on our jobs. Without me, it all falls apart.

Now, 6 teas, 4 with 2 sugars, 2 without... or 3 without? 2 coffees, one black, no, both white...
Dammit! Another project management meeting needed.

ANIMALS

A Chocolate Lab-romance (Ian)

The Pongo and Perdy of the Chocolate Labrador world meet, but their lab-romance is stymied by doggy differences.

Perdy tiptoes daintily along trails; Pongo ploughs recklessly through bushes. Perdy, head held high, is elegance personified; shoulders down, ears flapping, Pongo's all tongue and slobber. Perdy is angular, pretty, her body sleek, lean; Pongo's a fridge on legs, head like a butcher's block with a snout.

They sniff, then one trots and the other lollops away, Perdy an oasis of daffodils to cavort about in; Pongo to plunge headfirst into a manky stream.

Neither, it seems, pushed the other's chocolate buttons.

Foxy (Ian)

The fox must have sat in my garden for a good two minutes, waiting and watching as I fumbled in my pocket for my phone.

He shook his head in wry amusement as I tried to remember my code.

A canine eyebrow raised as I opened my camera app. (Yes, he knew that I didn't know the quick way). He chortled as I frantically swiped between camera settings.

Finally, as I pressed record, he strolled away with a huge foxy smirk on his face.

He had a lovely bushy tail.

The tip is less bushy… as my video sadly shows.

Time for Plan B (Ian)

The hive in crisis, the Queen called a meeting. There was a predictable buzz of anticipation as she entered the grand chamber.

'We all know we have a problem,' she began. 'Nectar collection is down fifty percent. Our brave worker bees are being picked off by those dratted birds because their bright stripes are easy to see. As you know, we decided to change outfits. We tried the spots but they were worse. Now... I'm afraid we've no other choice.'

There was a gasp as a dour-looking, brown, stripeless bee entered the chamber.

'We have to go to plain bee.'

Horsing Around (Ian)

'Ian – no *horsey jokes* or else!' read an email recently from someone trying to *stirrup* trouble. Some *unstable* correspondent, no doubt.

Furlong time now, I've wanted to prove the *saddle* folks – the *neigh-sayers* - that my knowledge of *horsey-colt-ur*e is as good as anyone's. In the *mane*, I'm never one to *shire* way from a challenge. But I'll not just *trot* out anything, *de-canter* load of tired horse jokes.
I'm no *foal*.

I'm *filly* committed. Ready... under *starter's orders*...

Wait - just in! Another *request-re-Ian*...
It says I'm a *nag*!

You want me to stop? You sure?

Yes, *Horse-shoe do.*

Riley Rhino's Really Rough Ride (Ian)

First day at the local crash and young Riley wasn't a happy rhino.

'They called me blockhead,' he said to Mum on the way home.
'Never mind, dear.'
'Said my ears were too small.'
'Ignore them, dear.'
'Piggy eyes, they reckoned I had.'
'Calves are cruel, dear.'
'Stumpy legs. I haven't got stumpy legs, have I, Mum?'
'Well…'
'They teased me because I didn't have a horn.'
'It'll grow, dear.'
'And they didn't like it when I charged about everywhere. That's what we're supposed to do, isn't it?'
'You need to be more thick-skinned.'
'Oh, no! Not you as well!'

The Place he Hoped he'd Never See Again (Ian)

He'd sat at the desk, staring at the words on the page. Just lines and dots, yet the message had been clear: he was to return to the place he hoped he'd never see again.

A chance to heal wounds? Not for him.

Angry and scared, he put up a fight. In the end, he had no choice. As the engine roared into life, he stared forward, desperate not to go, helpless to prevent it. Fear, worry, he used to have the balls to face it all. Now... only scars.

Check-up, bloody vets. Ought to be a law against neutering.

PHILOSOPHY

And the Moral to the Story is... (Ian)

Well, that was a bloody stupid idea!

What made you think that 'slow and steady' was ever going to be a long-term strategy for winning races? He mullered me second time round, proving that if you have long legs, lightning-fast reactions and a simple plan NOT to fall asleep again halfway round, it's quite easy to beat a tortoise. I lost by a country mile. Humiliating! A complete and utter disaster, and it's all your fault. You and your holier than thou moralising. Everything has to have meaning, doesn't it?

Well, here's some wise words for you, Aesop:

Sod off!

All Aboard the Blindingly Obvious Metaphor for Life (Ian)

At birth, you emerge from the tunnel with a loud whoo-whoo!... a-nnnn-d... you're off, down the track of life. *Clickety-clack, clickety-clack.* A youngster's smile at Thomas the Tank Engine, too soon becomes a teenage obsession with Platform 9 and 3/4 as you hurtle through childhood. *Clickety-clack, clickety-clack.* Inter-railing round Europe. La *clickety-clack, la clickety-clack.* Full steam ahead into adulthood. Clickety-clack. A Brief Encounter with love, a sad farewell. *Clickety-clack.* Change here for the gravy train. *Clickety-clack.* Running out of steam. *Click...ety...cl...ack.* End of the line.

Recently departed, you become another eternal sleeper on the track of life.

Clickety-clack, clickety-clack. Clickety-clunk.

Come the Resolution (Ian)

He resolved never to wear socks, give up his dummy or eat what he didn't like.

He resolved not to go round the supermarket without screaming or to be strapped into his car seat without bucking.

He resolved not to shower on demand or brush his teeth for 2 minutes.

He resolved not to give up toys or to lose games well.

He resolved never to be at school on time, sit quietly or to be told.

He resolved never to listen to lies or to be intimidated.

He resolved never to be silenced.

Come the resolution.

Come the revolution.

Dramatic Exit (Ian)

My brother-in-law, the salesman, was on a high. The presentation had been slick, effective and very well received. The account was in the bag, no doubt about it

Buzzing with adrenalin, he made his way towards the boardroom door, shaking hands with the whole team, smiling and joking as he said his farewells.

One last enthusiastic wave and a promise to see them all very soon, before he walked through the door... straight into the stationery cupboard.

The moral of the story?

If you're going to make a dramatic exit, just remember you might have to come back in again.

The Guardian of Time (Ian)

'Do you have to keep repeating yourself?' she said.

'Yes,' he said. 'It's my job.'

'Your job? It's hardly a job, is it?'

'You're right. More like a calling.'

'A calling? Sitting around clockwatching?'

'I'm the Guardian of Time. It's an important role.'

'You say that, but it shouldn't stop you doing other things. I could do with a hand cleaning this place.'

'Don't fuss. There's only us... and THE clock, of course... There goes another minute. Tick-tock. Tick-tock'

'Do you have to keep repeating yourself?' she said.

'Yes,' he said. 'It's my job.'

'Your job?' It's hardly a job...'

PLACES

Castles in the Air (Ian)

It's a little-known fact that castles were often built far away. This was to make them look smaller than they actually were.

Attackers would approach the castle in question, confident its size was no threat. By the time they realised it was massive, it was too late and the castle guard would be upon them, shouting, 'Fooled you!'

Colchester Castle is one of the very few that were built close by. Historians claim this is either because the Normans believed its thick walls were impregnable or, more likely, that they wanted to be handy for the bus station and Keddies.

Hysterical Colchester (Ian)

Colchester is full of history. There is a plaque in town of the 'Crouched Friars', so called because this religious sect adopted the 'knees bent' rather than the more painful 'stooped' position method when frying their food.

And did you know that history was discovered in the late 1990s by the first ever historian, Luke Bach-Woods? During an architectural dig under Colchester Castle, he discovered an ancient tomb full of history books with dates and events, neatly set out for children to learn, most of which are still forgotten today.

Fake history, of course, was around long before fake news.

Into the Night (Ian)

Handpicked from the tribe by the queen's champion, the Hendos were mighty warriors – loyal, determined heroines all – on a quest for glory.

They stalked the ancient city streets, searching high and low, perpetually on the lookout, forever diligent, seeking that one opportunity to open the gates to paradise.

Across cobbled stones they marched, over rivers, up tight narrow staircases, through dark alleyways, ready to act, dressed to kill. Until finally, exhausted, there it was: The Golden Grail.

'You're not coming in here in that state,' said its landlord in his thick Edinburgh accent. 'Hen do or no bloody hen do.'

The Saga of Townsend Thoreson (Ian)

Townsend Thoreson stood exhausted aside the Castle, his comrades scattered about him. His quest from Copenhagen to Colchester was over.

For one whole day and no nights, he had strove, strived or striven (he was never sure which) to lead his compatriots to that holiest of places, The Fleece, only to discover it had been smoted (smote, smited?) and replaced by the Halifax Building Society.

On their odyssey, they had conquered several Essex undulations and bested many other obstacles (trials, roadworks). Their bounty? Nothing but the taste of bitter disappointment... and, no disappointing bitter either to taste.

A right saga.

Which Way to Narnia? (Ian)

A rustle of the sheets as, after a heavy night out, he got out of bed, heading she assumed, for the toilet.

She listened for the front door; he had history of lumbering through the wrong one. There was a bang – not a toilet door bang. She dashed into the hallway, relieved to see the front door still on the chain, but the bathroom was empty.

A thud from the closed cupboard revealed his whereabouts. There he was, barely able to fit, face hard against the boiler.

A drunken smile and then he slurred: 'I appear to have been misdirected.'

RELATIONSHIPS

My Sullen Valentine (Ian)

Furious, she told him he'd forgotten. Again! Why he didn't put a reminder on his phone, she didn't know. Trouble was, he didn't care enough.

Bemused, he asked what he'd forgotten.

An incredulous look. Perhaps some clues might help? The near-empty Chardonnay in the fridge? He shrugged. A plastic rose between her teeth? A headshake. The menu from the letter rack? Um... The last Christmas Quality Street? Zilch. A spray of Coco Chanel? Nope.

Finally, exasperated, she threw the lot to the floor and stormed out

Bottles, flowers, piece of paper, wrappings, something smelly. All discarded... Got it!

Bin day

The High-life (Ian)

'Women are too good for you,' your mother used to snarl.

Her nastiness tipped you over the edge. Provoking you to tip her over the edge – twenty floors up.

You decide to prove her wrong.

'No strings attached,' you tell your dates. But killing proves habitual. They perish, pushed from on high.

No strings attached? They wish there had been.

You get cocky. The next that falls for you, will fall for you from the top of the Shard.

You meet... you are smitten.

Until she tips you over the edge.

Your mother was right: women are too good for you.

I'm All Shook Up (Ian)

We had a tiff. She rocked and I rolled.

'You're obsessed with Elvis,' she thrust.

'You're saying he's *Always on My Mind*?' I parried.

'Give it up,' she swiped.

'*Don't Be Cruel*,' I lunged, 'I need this opportunity. It's *Now or Never*.'

'Elvis comes first in your priority list!' she punched.

'Not true,' I blocked. '*He's Way Down*, compared to you.'

'Don't believe you,' she stabbed.

'That's your *Suspicious Mind*.'

'We need marriage counselling' her uppercut.

'Honestly, I'd prefer *A Little Less Conversation*,' I pouted.

Wow! Such banter. I called her *The Devil in Disguise*. But she's really an *Angel*.

Top Dog (Ian)

He had to be first. First in line. First for lunch. First in tests. First to get changed, sit down, stand up. First in games and races. Always first.

Until he wasn't.

First to anger. First to cheat. First to throw a punch.

First to trouble. First to rebel, to leave home... to disappoint.

First to join a gang, to deal, to mug, to rob.

First in the bank. First to the safe. First to the cash.

Always first. Until he wasn't.

Last out the bank. Last to drop the gun. Last to be shot.

Last breath... first – 'I'm sorry.'

ROYALS

A Disappointment (Glad)

The King and Queen were coming to the Essex Show, and the whole school was going to be there. This was 1948, with no television, so to actually see them...wow!

We made Union Jack flags and, on the day, set off for our place on the route. The road was lined with excited adults and children.

At last, the traffic stopped, the road was empty. Cheers gradually got louder, then 2 policemen arrived on motorbikes followed by a large car. Inside were 2 ordinary people waving.

But where were the golden carriages, horses, soldiers, the king and queen wearing crowns?

Queen Brenda - Circa 30AD to Circa 60 AD (Ian)

Queen Brenda Seer (aka Brenda Kerr) will be remembered for her influential role in the Norfolk band 'Iceni'.

Previously managed by Colin 'The Celt' Prasutugus (Gus to his friends), the group struggled to get a foothold on the Britannia scene until Brenda became lead vocalist. Her ability to network (she loved gate crashing toga parties) and uncompromising approach slayed audiences. Grand entrances at gigs on a chariot, waving a spear, shouting 'Death to the Romans' were not popular marketing tactics with everyone, but Brenda and her tribe stormed Camulodunum and the southeast, lighting up venues everywhere.

Rebel with a cause.

Addendum

Queen Brenda Seer leaves behind 200,000 dead warriors, a temple in ruins and a reputation for not being messed with.

A Special Occasion (Ian)

The Che Guevara T-shirt is perfect. Trousers are tight and might squeak, but the leather says I'm down with the kids AND sexy. Hair looks sharp. I'm pleased with the mullet. Baseball cap – on backwards, naturally. Trainers – Nike. A bit flash but they're so comfy! Earbuds in - I'll need my tunes on. Gold chain, fake Rolex, and skull ring finish it off. Yep, I'm ready.

Oh… mustn't forget the Incredible Hulk underpants that Mummy got me.

Velvet robe and ermine cape over the top.

Just need to remember to hold onto my crown when the Red Arrows fly over.

CHRISTMAS

Sam Saves Christmas (Ian)

Uncle Colin – boastful, brash, liar – was in full flow. 'How I saved Christmas'– a story of driving around Europe, delivering toys to the poor.

Lies! He couldn't drive, hadn't been further than Calais and always spent Christmas week drunk in his local.

Sam had had enough. '£50 says you can't eat a sprout,' he challenged.

A gasp around the table – no one had ever eaten one of Aunty Pauline's sprouts.

'Fifty? Okay!'

They watched in silence.   Sprout to mouth... swallow... Pause... gag... End of Uncle Colin.

'Sorry, Aunty Pauline,' Sam said solemnly.

'That's alright... Can I have his fifty quid?'

A Christmas Craic (Ian)

Snowbound, Scrooge was stuck in a Cork hotel. 'Bah, humbug,' he moaned to Jacob who was supping a Guinness in the lobby.

'Cheer up, Ebenezer. It's the Glow Cork Celebration.'

'What's that?'

'The Christmas lights... in Oliver Plunkett Street and Grand Parade – beautiful! Oh, and there's the English Market and Lucey Park illuminations! Hayfield Manor Hotel's display's stunning and the view from the river...'

'Sounds dreadful.'

'Well, I'm up for the craic.'

'What's that?'

'Irish for great company... lively conversation... fun... enjoyment'

'What's that?'

'I'm off out, Scrooge,' said Jacob downing his pint and leaving. 'I'll let the ghosts explain.'

Daddy Claus (Glad)

'Miss... Andrew said that there's no Father Christmas,' Daniel pined.

My class of 6-year-olds suddenly went very quiet.

'Who told you that?' Michelle called out.

'My mum,' replied Andrew.

30 pairs of eyes gazed up at me. My dilemma? Andrew's parents always believed in telling him the truth - how could I disagree with them? But, conversely, how could I face the disappointment of 29 children ... and their parents?

Then Daniel asked, 'Who brings us our presents then?'

'Your dad,' replied Andrew.

'Don't be daft, Andrew. How could my dad get all round the world in just one night?'

HEALTH

Hugs (Glad)

`

At 7.45pm, the bell would ring. I'd leave my wife to line up outside the nursery window, with other new fathers, waiting to see our new-born children.

'Name?'

A tiny bundle, face scarcely visible – was presented at the window. That was it for ten days our wives were in hospital after giving birth. No holding, cuddling, cooing. That came later.

As that baby grew from a child to a woman, there were tears, laughter... but always hugs.

Covid, and now I am on the other side of the window. Wheeled – presented – to my grown-up baby.

Full circle to no hugs.

The Wee Small Hours (Ian)

For me, after midnight is called the 'wee small hours' for good reason. My bladder never sleeps, though other monsters awaken me too.

The smoke alarm beeps – like its owner, in need of new batteries.

Outside, the security light flashes while foxes frolic.

The plumbing – trapped air in pipes – gurgles, splutters, whines. I should change my diet.

A by-product of sleeping – snoring – rouses me. How ironic! How cruel.

Doors bang as the bathroom entices others, and I'm up again.

We cross... ships that piss in the night.

The good news? I'm well on my way to 10,000 steps before dawn.

The Message (Glad)

At last! The message I'd been waiting for. Just a time and place... but I knew it was from THEM.

I contacted the rest of the group - no one had heard. I was the first!

Only 3 more days - excited, fearful, but I knew it was right. So many questions - Exact location? Who was in charge? How would they recognise me?

The big day. Bang on time, I arrived. A masked man directed me to the back of the building. More people in masks, eyes visible, tense, muffled voices.

More waiting... Until finally...

A jab! My vaccine for Covid19!

Bed Sobs and Room Stinks (Ian)

'How's life on the ward, grandad?'

'Bloody awful. It's like a zoo. Bed 1 in the corner snores like a klaxon. Bed 2 keeps having a pee in the bin. The one opposite shouts in his sleep.'

'What about the ones in the beds either side?'

'He sings sea shanties, and that one doesn't stop crying. As for bed 6 by the door… the smell!'

'It seems quiet at the moment.'

'Yes, deathly quiet.'

'Grandad… you haven't been raiding the dispensary again, have you? They'll get suspicious.'

'No!… Well, yes… maybe… Return that bottle on your way out, will you?'

The New Norma (Ian)

When it's over, Norma says we shall wear pyjama bottoms outside. Toilet paper will replace Bitcoin. We shall spontaneously jump sideways into the road. The letter 'R' will be a letter again and not a number.

'Hello' will be replaced by 'you're-on-mute'. When we meet in person, we shall lean forward, peer quizzically, smile broadly and wave enthusiastically in each other's faces.

Amazon parcels will again be left in bins or behind gates. We won't sing happy birthday without washing our hands. We shall no longer bake, garden or exercise.

This is Norma. She is new and we will follow.

The Missing Hearing Aid

(A true story about Glad, written by Ian)

You search high, you search low. You ransack the bed, throwing duvet and cover on the floor, shaking pillow cases, the sheet, your head, despondently. The washing doesn't escape your scrutiny, nor your coat pockets, shoes, slippers, your hat and scarf, discarded on the table.

On hands and knees, you go, peering underneath cupboards, the sofa, the bed (again)... the cat. You sweep the floor with eyes and broom, rummage through bins and drawers, searching high and low, in vain.

It's gone, definitely gone. Until you discover with relief – while relieving – that it hasn't.

Next time, check your knickers first.

The Deathbed (Ian)

'Not long now,' the GP announced to the family.

The man had lived a long, largely happy life. Lovely family, travel, good job, friends. The only blot? His GP's recommendation thirty years previously to give up red wine when blotches appeared on his skin. He'd really loved his red wine.

The GP responded magnanimously to the thanks for the care he had given.

'My only bad call was the whole red wine thing.'

A twitch from the bed.

'I've since found out that it was cucumber skin that caused it.'

They died together, the man's hands around the GP's throat.

The Lockdown the Walks and the Wardrobe

(Again, about Glad, written by Ian)

Every morning during lockdown, my 80-year-old mum walked, wearing outfits from her imaginary wardrobe.

Friends, family awaited the emails. What would she pick that day? Who would she be? Winston, Batman, Cleopatra? Flatfooted, moustached cane twirling; puffing a huge cigar with fingers in a V? Her curtains a dress now, alive with the sound of music; number six on her back, the world cup aloft perhaps? Parrot squawking on her shoulder, small steps round the house, giant leaps for womankind.

Crowned, booted, bejewelled – a Dalek in a wig? A masked crusader – a superhero in lockdown... with underpants over her tights.

ENTERTAINMENT

Saturday Morning Pictures (Glad)

The highlight of the week was Saturday morning pictures. No T.V. back then. Cinema was jam-packed with children. Only adults were the grumpy manager and long-suffering usherettes.

The noise from the audience was louder than the films! Shouts, whistles, groans if the hero showed sentiment. Films were Cowboys and Indians, a couple of cartoons and, of course, the likes of Laurel and Hardy, Charlie Chaplin. Sweets were on rationing, so no food or drink.

This was our entertainment. We were always amazed to emerge and find it light outside.

And then we played Cowboys and Indians all the way home!

Strictly Dad Dancing (Ian)

'Welcome to the audition. Can you dance, Mr 'Hornett?'

Of course, I can dance. I have:

Played air guitar to Bat Out of Hell in Terry's lounge.

Rocked shoulders 'All Over the World'.

Swayed 'cooly' to Bob Marley.

Clucked elbows to The Birdie Song at French campsites.

Hokey-cokeyed.

Mashed potatoes.

Time warped.

Twisted.

Pogo-ed.

Shuffled feet self-consciously at Junior School discos.

Oops Upsided my head on beer-stained floors.

Done the Lambeth Walk (and shouted 'Oi')

Turned the right way once doing the Macarena.

Waved my arms about to the MYCA.'

'Come now, is that dancing, Mr Hornett?'

'Er, strictly?... no.'

Dick Barton - Special Agent (Glad)

Back in the day...No televisions, computers, mobile phones, or record players. Our entertainment was playing in the street.

There were few cars to interfere with games. Cricket had dustbins as wickets, the football owner always the captain, and every house had a front garden to hide in. Players came and went, called in to eat, rejoining later. It never spoilt the game.

But there was a radio programme that stopped play for everyone. 6.45 Monday to Friday. The 'Devil's Gallop' signalled the start of Dick Barton Special agent.

The street would empty and we rushed indoors.15 minutes of pure escapism.

Flight or Plight (Ian)

Flight Club – raucous crowds, banging music, fun darts games.

Game three looks simple: aim for one. Points if you hit it, two points for a double, three for a treble. My first set… I miss everything. The next set, treble one first dart!

'Two!' my teammates shout, demanding a second. 'Two!'

I aim, throw… Another treble one! The crowd go wild – two consecutive trebles!

'Two!' they celebrate. 'Two!'

I blank out the noise, aim… it's in! Three treble ones – what a guy! I turn to acknowledge my teammates.

'Two, you bloody idiot. You were supposed to aim for the two!'

Fashion Sense (Ian)

'Love your outfit!'

'You taking the mick?'

'Only banter. Anyway, I can't talk – look at me. Stethoscope with beachwear. I'm supposed to be an airhostess.'

'The flippers are an unusual touch. That's your plane, then?'

'Yep. That your tank?'

'Yep.'

'Why...'

'Why am I wearing a spacesuit? Lord knows.'

'Cowboy hat's weird.'

'Perched on top of the helmet too.'

'How can I get into role dressed like this?'

'It's impossible, I agree... I'm Humphrey, by the way.'

'Never imagined Action Man being a Humphrey.'

'You're Barbie.'

'How'd you...? Oh... she's put me back in the sodding box again, hasn't she?'

EDUCATION

The Class Pet (Glad)

The hamster was a much-loved friend in my class of 6-year-olds. With parents' permission, a child could take him home for the weekend. Friday lunchtime was spent cleaning Hammy's cage and explaining his care.

Gary wanted him, but having heard nothing from his mum, I asked that she see me.

'We would love to have the hamster, but we don't have much luck with animals.'

'Really?' I said.

'Yeah, I hoovered up the last hamster we had.'

'Oh, dear.'

'Yeah, and it wasn't until the dog fell off the sofa that I realised the kids had glued his paws together!'

Kids Today (Ian)

'I want to use today's lesson to recap on the grammar terms we've learnt so far.

Let's start with the basics: what's a prepositional phrase?... No?... Okay, let's break it down. What's a preposition?... A phrase?... You can't remember... Never mind. Let's move on... Write a sentence with a main clause and a subordinate clause... Yes, of course there's a difference... No, you can't go to the toilet... Rewrite this sentence using the passive voice... yes... passive. Come on, we did this yesterday!

Right, that's it! If this remote learning's going to work, you need to learn this stuff... Dad.'

NO SMOKING! (Glad)

Back in the day, when smoking was acceptable, some parents while waiting to collect their children from our Infants school would have a cigarette in the entrance lobby, thus causing smoke to drift around the school. They would also leave cigarette butts on the floor. So, a NO SMOKING sign was put up.

We often had visits from former pupils who had moved on to the junior school

'Why have you put that notice up?' asked Samantha quizzically.

'To stop smoking and smoke in the school.'

'We don't have to do that. None of the kids in the Juniors smoke.'

Tell Me Why (Ian)

Teachers teach the 5Ws to children in English lessons. Who, what, where, when and why are guaranteed to help budding journalists get to the bottom of any story.

Less effective when teachers try to practise what they preach. The following 5Ws, regularly used, are guaranteed to illicit baffled shrugs and absolutely no information what – or indeed, who, where, why and when - soever.

'Who do you think you are?'

'What do you think you're doing?'

'And where might you be going?'

'When will you come to your senses?'

And the most useless of all:

'Explain yourself... just tell me... why?'

The Awards Ceremony (Ian)

An expectant buzz in the audience, anticipation is high.

Two strong contenders.

Two massive egos.

One coveted prize.

Glory for the winner.

Side by side they sit, thoughts bombard their brains:

'I've got this.'

'He has no chance.'

'Her work is sloppy.'

'He's so lazy.'

'She doesn't deserve it.'

'No talent at all.'

Sideway glances, false smiles. 'I love your work,' he says.

'And I love yours,' she replies.

'You're very kind.'

'So are you.'

'Good luck,' they say together.

Finally... The noise dies down. Then, a hush.

The result is in…

'And year 3's Star of the Week is…'

MODERN DAY LIVING

Mister Blaster (Ian)

Washed up, too old, out of touch? Not down with the kids? He'd show them he still had his finger on the pulse, his ear to the streets. He was Mr Cool: the main man.

He'd needed help lifting it onto his shoulder, but now he was upright, balanced, ready to go. Spotify, smartphones, Bluetooth earpieces – they could take a running jump.

With sunglasses, baseball cap, a rucksack full of cassette tapes, and the emergency number for his chiropractor in his back pocket, Reggie teetered, then moseyed down the drive, Wham cranked up – full volume – blaring from his ghetto blaster.

Technology Turmoil (Glad)

Internet banking's simple and more convenient.

Telephone call connects me to a charming man to guide me through on my iPad.

Problems immediately...

Set up security number - Where's the keyboard gone?

Create password - Oh no, another one!

Security questions to establish I am who I say I am - What did I say when setting up the account?

User name - What does that mean?

More questions - to complete and remember.

After an hour, set up app – A what? Finally, finished.

'Anything else I can do for you today?'

'Well, I do need some milk and bread.'

Pilates Mat For Sale (Ian)

Breathe in.'   *I breathe out.*
'Not out, in!'   *I breathe in.*
'That's it. Leg out.'   *Which leg?*
'The left... no, the left.'   *That is my... Apologies... that's my left.*
'Hold it and breathe in.'   *I haven't breathed out yet!*
'And hold...'   *My leg or my breath?*
'And in... no, bring your leg in.'   *In? Bring it in how?*
'And out. No, keep your leg in, breathe out.'   *Leg out, breathe in?*
'Stomach in.'   *And breathe out?*
'Leg out.'   *Out again?*
'Breathe in, and hold...'   *Hold what?*
'And out...'   *She's taking the mick.*
'And... relax...'   *Relax, she says. Relax!*
... I'm out!

Number 5 (Glad)

Sainsburys had just opened. I was warned about the size of the car park and to remember where I park. I noted number 5 on the lane, and continued to the store and shopping.

When I came out, the car park was completely full, but confidently, I made my way to lane 5. I walked up and down, searching, but no car!

Convinced my car was stolen, I returned to the store, glancing along the lanes as I went. Each lane was marked 5 miles per hour!

It was another half hour before me and my trolley found my car.

Love at First Megabyte (Ian)

His screen lit up with delight when he spotted her. Sleek, neat, she sat on the table in a corner, oblivious to the effect she was having on his algorithms. 'Open dating app,' he instructed his owner. Powerless to resist, he obliged. 'Search Samsung Galaxy Ultra.' With one of the best blueteeth around, connection took a nanosecond. As for compatibility... functionality and a massive RAM would impress. The app did its thing and their owners met.

'My name's Iphone15pro... can I buy you a data boost?' he said.

Smart talk between Smartphones. This was internet dating at a cellular level.

The Warning (Ian)

A warning, in no uncertain terms: half-an-hour, then... that's it. Nothing. A mad rush follows. Keyboard is frantically tapped – attempts to put things right, make contact, pass on the warnings. Let others know that... well... just let them know. A chance to say hello... maybe. Certainly, no time for goodbyes. Hope fades.

The clock ticks down. Too soon, it's too late. It goes quiet. Not a word. Sitting, waiting now – unsure what to do. There's nothing to do.

The warning was right...

Two hours bloody internet's down. Three Zoom meetings ruined. Takeaway order lost. And I missed most the cricket!

What's In Store? (Ian)

Prefer to stand in line rather than sit online? Earache from excessive mouse clicking? Concerned your eyes will ever stop scrolling up and down? Is your voice hoarse from shouting thanks at departing delivery vans? Hopes for the planet crushed with the acres of cardboard used to deliver your toothpaste?

If the answer to any of these questions is 'yes' then you have come to the right place!

For the very best in Colchester retail, try our fully interactive experience, guaranteed to open doors. You never know: you might even meet a human!

Shops – Try them today! While stores last.

Meditation (Ian)

'Deep breaths... close your eyes... aware of the space around you.'

He loves meditation.

'Relax... follow your breath...' *So relaxing*

'Clear your mind.' *Mind's clear.*

'Nothing to think about.' *Nothing at all.*

'In... and...' *Baked beans! Put it on the list.*

'...out...and in...' *That gate's banging again.*

'... and out...' *B&Q do hinges.*

'... and in...' *Tom! Yes, that's his name... got it.*

... 2 nil – lost again.

... That Email's worrying.

... Sausages maybe?

... Brexit!

... Or was it, Tim?

... Could wedge the gate.

... Or a nice bit of a fish?

... Rain later.

'... And open your eyes.'

Why does he bother?

HOLIDAYS

The Holiday (Glad)

It was their first 'proper' holiday. There had been little spare money with 5 children to raise. Now they were all off hand and they decided to go to a holiday camp.

No food to cook, chalet cleaned and all entertainment laid on - it was wonderful! They joined in all the daytime activities, then off to the ballroom for the evening's festivities.

On their return home, they couldn't wait to tell their children about it, especially Mum taking part in the singing contest. 'The audience loved it didn't they, Tom?'

'Yes, he said. 'You could have heard a bomb drop!'

Around the World in 100 Words (Ian)

My driveway, Mile End Road, Colchester. First decision: left, or right? I go left. Past North Station, A12 southwest. Travel the breadth of England, Wales, over the Irish Sea. Scoot though the Emerald Isle, splash across the Atlantic, whizz through the States. Next, the Pacific to China. Lost! Take first left to India, sail to Oman, trek up through Saudi Arabia, Egypt.

Pasta in Sicily, cheeky bistro in Paris. Chips on the ferry from the Hook to Harwich. Down the A120... end of Mill Road.

Finally, there! Pint in the Dog and Pheasant.

Should've gone right, though. Much, much quicker.

Suspicious Activity (Glad)

We were at a secluded villa in France, one dwelling nearby. No friendly waves or attempts to converse by the inhabitants. Doors silently closed, hushed voices, car boots clicked shut. After a day out, we'd sit on the lawn with our drinks, surreptitiously watching the house. There was something fishy going on.

One evening, we settled with our glasses of wine, staring at the house. Then we spied a shotgun at the window!

We froze, waiting to become statistics. The door opened... we watched her walk out... holding the hose of a Hoover, ready to empty it into the bin.

Hunting Waterfalls (Ian)

The Douro Valley, Portugal. We're hunting waterfalls. 5 adults, 5 pairs of walking shoes, 5 terrified expressions. The sign says to take care. No barriers, no guides, no sense. However, it's stunning. Waterfall upon waterfall, cascading over rocks into a myriad of glistening pools. So, tempting. So dangerous.

Tentatively, we pick our way down, heading for a sumptuous spot 100 metres below. Clinging on, stepping over channels with sheer drops, we caution, encourage, take no risks... and follow the guy in flip-flops, carrying a freezer box in one hand, deckchairs in the other, and a 3-year-old perched on his shoulders.

The Edge of the Outback (Ian)

The edge of the outback, 90 degrees, no shade, scorched earth, hot heads. Our only means of sustenance? 5 dozen cans of Tooheys beer, 10kg of steaks, 20 rolls, and a bucket of coleslaw. No matches, so igniting the barbie was an issue.

Fortunately, Clive was on hand to save the day.

'I can get a fire going anywhere, anytime,' he boasted.

Recently arrived in Oz, I stood back, pleased to hear that ancient aboriginal skills were influencing modern thinking. A second later, the bag of charcoal was roaring.

And it had only taken one short burst from Clive's flamethrower.

TRAVEL

Surprise on the Orient Express (Glad)

A letter from the BBC arrived explaining that a programme marking the 70th anniversary of the Venice Simplon Orient Express would be made by The BBC Holiday programme. Our names had been chosen at random with 6 other previous passengers. If we were willing to be interviewed, we would spend a weekend on the iconic train and be photographed for their next brochure.

Excited, I spent the next hours, phoning family, planning new clothes and how to lose that 2 stone!

Looked again at the letter for the address, noticed the date: APRIL 1st.

April-fooled Chris had wreaked his revenge!

A P-riceless True Story (Ian)

Spain-dwelling Malcolm was set for a pleasant evening with family at the Chinese restaurant. Despite limited common language between Malcolm and waitress, the order was made and dishes soon appeared.

But Malcolm was not happy. 'No rice?' he said, pointing to the rice-less table before them 'No rice?'

The waitress nodded her understanding and went on her way.

The food kept coming. With each batch came the frustrated cry, 'No rice? No rice?' followed by the nod and... no rice.

'I didn't get what I asked for,' Malcolm moaned later.

Malcolm, you got exactly what you asked for: NO RICE!

(With thanks to Sean Clements and his dad for the story).

Dust (Ian)

For days she trudged. Through thick forests, navigating freezing streams and rivers, across rocks and blistering hot sand. The air thinned and her lungs laboured as the terrain steepened.

She pushed on.

Screed held her up with the end in sight. Ten metres gained, only for five to be lost. Eventually, exhausted, she reached the plateau, just as the tiny particles wafted down from the heavens, settling on her shoulders, in her hair, all over until she was covered from head to toe.

Then she too became dust, to be wafted away through the ether to the next distant sun.

Billy's Roots (Ian)

Poor Elsie couldn't cope after her beloved died of pleurisy. A seamstress, she left for the States to work, leaving baby Billy in Cork with great Aunt Tess and Uncle Jack. For five years, childless, they worshipped Billy, loved and cherished him - hid him when Elsie returned to whisk him Stateside. Fought for him. Gave him up, devastated, when the courts decreed.

Elsie? Had her happiness... at last.

Tess and Jack? Had theirs... before it disappeared.

Billy? Seasickness for 5 days and a lifetime in the Land of Opportunity.

But he had his roots in the Emerald Isle... forever.

IAN HORNETT

I Did It (Glad)

I knew I could do it! The weeks of waiting, wondering if I would fail at the last minute.

Now all the formalities have been completed, I am through. There is no turning back. I have to sit and wait watching the clock, surrounded by a milling crowd of unknown faces trying to calm myself until I am called.

Hands clenched tight, sweating. Until, at last, I make my way to the queue and then up the stairs to my seat. I did it! I'm on the plane!

But you are not there to soothe me and hold my hand.

Return Trip (Ian)

'Hi! How was the trip?' he asked, taking a welcome sip from his lemonade.

It was hot, mainly blue sky, fluffy clouds floated serenely across the sky.

She sighed. 'Not good. I didn't get as much out of it as I hoped.'

'Remind me: where did you go?'

'Here and there, but mainly Bognor.'

'What was wrong with it?'

'It was mainly Bognor.'

'You wouldn't go back?'

'Nah'

'How long did you stay?'

'Just the 72 years. Bus got me.'

'Ouch! Where next?'

'Anywhere but Bognor.'

'I'll have a word.'

'Appreciate it.'

'No sweat. Next?...

Hi! How was the trip?'

FOOD & DRINK

Gobstoppers (Glad)

Tightly clutching our pennies, we raced to the sweet shop. A bell announced our arrival. We stared at shelves of glass jars full of our favourite sweets: aniseed balls, blackjacks, barley sugar jelly babies. What to buy?

Lemon sherbet to lick until our tongues were yellow, pear drops sucked until roofs of mouths sore, maybe even a mars bar? Eager faces watched as the shopkeeper weighed our weekly sweet treat.

But best of all was the gobstopper! So big it hardly fitted our little mouths! Shared with friends, taking turns sucking while it changed colour and grew smaller and smaller.

Potato Head (Glad)

There were few ways to cook potatoes: boil or roast, plus an occasional bag of chips. Bonfire night a potato was pushed into the fire to emerge an hour later with black, crinkled skin, then hungrily devoured, our cheeks red from the dying fire.

Now potatoes have become sophisticated. New potatoes available all year, different varieties for those exotic dishes: au gratin, boulangere, lyonnaise, croutons, rosti, and jacket potatoes with a variety of fillings. No longer just a vegetable to fill you, but a force of its own.

Even Mr Potato Head has become gender neutral. Now called Potato Head.

Respect (Ian)

Cocky Bernard would show off when out with friends.

'Have you tried cooking it before you serve it?'

'Change the table cloth. I'm allergic to cotton.'

'Chopsticks? I'm not a heathen.'

'My Sambuca is corked.'

'Tell me: did you always want to wipe tables when you grew up?'

'Mocha: Guernsey full fat milk. You do have Turbinado sugar? You don't know what that is? Tea then. You CAN pour water over a bag?'

He would laugh condescendingly... and leave with a sneer.

But alone in lockdown, Cocky Bernard's wings were clipped.

Now he smiles gratefully... and leaves a hefty tip.

The Legend of Boomer (Ian)

A heavy drinking session in the Peldon Rose and Andy was feeling slightly worse for wear.

Thoughtful friends gave him a lift to his house down the road, placed him fast asleep on the sofa and left for the pub to rejoin the party. No sooner had they walked out than Andy awoke with a fierce thirst.

Reinvigorated, he jogged the hundred metres diagonally across the field behind his house, straight through the pub back door, and was in his seat with a pint as his lift walked back into the bar.

Boomer - the human boomerang and comeback king.

You Can Never Have Too Many Cakes (Glad)

I had a voucher for afternoon tea at the newly opened hotel. On arrival, we were seated in the resplendent dining room, given a menu to select our choice of tea, before a cake stand arrived with dainty sandwiches, scones, cream, jam, and fancy cakes.

At the end, several small cakes remained. Avoiding the eyes of the waiter, we carefully wrapped them in serviettes, and put them in our bags.

'Was everything alright for you, madam?'

'Lovely, but there was such a lot!'

'You did very well. Most of our customers don't finish. They take some home in a box.'

A Storm in a Teacup (Ian)

13th century Saint, Tetley of Wivenhoe, charged fishermen for predicting storms using teacups and seagulls. If seagulls ignored the tea, it was safe for fishermen to go to sea. If seagulls added milk and two sugars to the tea, it meant a storm was brewing. Only after the last fishing boat in Essex sunk during a squall off Mersea, did fishermen realise it was a big con.

The saint said it was a huge fuss about nothing, but couldn't think of a pithy phrase to express himself so was executed in 1247.

More tales on seabirds and gullibility next week.

Choices (Glad)

The meal was finished and I needed to use the facilities.

I saw signs to the toilets and made my way along corridors, down a flight of stairs and through many doors. Relieved, I made it to the final choice of doors: 'Guys' and 'Gals'.

Feeling more comfortable, I started back, trying to remember the stairs, corridors and doors in reverse. Once again, the final choice of doors, these unmarked. Voices from behind one. It had to be the dining room.

The look on my daughter's face when she saw me across the kitchen counter was a sight to behold!

Secrets (Glad)

I woke that morning feeling good. Then I remembered what I had done! Whatever made me do it? Still, it was a new day, nobody knew and I had hidden it well. I needed to try to forget it.

Had my toast and fruit juice, listened to the radio, then went for a walk. But it was there on my mind all the time. At home I kept busy all the while glancing to the place, I had hidden it. Then, I could hold back no longer... I opened the cupboard and ate my Mars Bar!

Oh well, diet tomorrow.

BODY

Hands (Glad)

What a marvel, those tiny baby hands, so perfect. The joy when they grasp. As they grow bigger, their dexterity at catching, carefully drawing and making things, and the safety of reaching up and holding on. The first shy tentative handhold of young love. Hands sweating and bitten nails awaiting exam results. Hands for work and play becoming stronger, nourished with creams, nail polish added. The tenderness of hands, stroking and soothing others.

But they change and are no longer perfect. Fingers bend, skin blemishes, strength decreases. But to be stroked and held by another hand is still a joy.

Double-digit Dick (Ian)

Life had dealt Double-digit Dick a bad hand.

Two bad hands.

First to go, right thumb whipped off by a lorry, hitching a ride out of town. Left thumb followed, hitching back in to hospital.

The pinkies next, crushed in a drunken bet. Tommy Frampton and the steamroller won.

Too fat for its ring, leftie ring finger was amputated by his doctor; the right by his neighbour's hedge cutter.

A cigar guillotine did for left index finger. Alone on that hand, Middle wilted and died.

Leaving two on his right, which Double-digit Dick waved back at life to excellent effect.

My Soundscape (Ian)

I close my eyes; I hear things around me.

The whine, whirr, rumble of the road sweeper. I imagine it dodging amongst the cars. The clang cling creak of the aerial. I imagine the wind rattling through the rooftop. The click, whoosh, roar of the boiler. I imagine it awakening, obeying its thermostatic master. The chat, chit, chatter of children. I imagine them skipping and smiling. The clink, clank, clunk of the washing machine. I imagine it swirling, cleansing the dirt away. The zing, hiss, whizz of tinnitus.

I imagine I've got superpowers and can hear dog whistles in Sydney.

SOME OF GLAD'S OTHER MEMORIES

Apple Picking

Sandwiches, drinks, boots – we make for the meeting place. The van arrives and in we pile, greeting the other mothers and children.

At the farm, we are given apple carriers before heading to the orchards with rows of trees and ladders. Voices echo across the field, mums fill their carriers to tip in the containers, one eye on their children happily playing.

The day wears on, carriers feel heavy, legs, backs ache, until, at last, the whistle signals the end of the day. Exhausted!

But that taste of a freshly picked apple on an autumn morning will never leave me.

The Shopping Parade

Before supermarkets, we shopped locally. Shops open 9 to 5:30, half day Thursday, closed Sunday.

Grocer for tins, sugar, dairy products etc. Greengrocer for fruit and veg. Everything tipped into our own special bag. Butchers' windows displayed meat on trays – a model pig or plastic foliage when closed. The enticing aroma of fresh bread from the bakers lured us in.

Then the fish shop! Fish artistically arranged on a long marble slab. In the middle, was a metal deep sided tray full of live eels! Sometimes an eel would slither over the side and wriggle out.

Stuff nightmares are made of...

Water Everywhere

Newlyweds, they moved into the old cottage which came with his job. It was ok, just needed TLC ... Except for the kitchen! It was bad: cracks on the walls, uneven floor and an old wash boiler for the laundry.

After he left for work, she decided to tackle the washing. Filled the boiler with water, washing powder, turned to full power, before adding the clothes. The kitchen filled with steam, water dripped down the walls, puddles on the floor.

Hair soaking and lank, then the back door opened.

'My boss is here and wants to meet you' he said...

Time Heals

Grief is different for everyone, but you have to move on. Clothes are sorted and sent to charities, the empty bed and chair are just other pieces of furniture. Decisions and holidays alone.

No longer angry when seeing couples out together, or tears without reason. No longer thinking that I must tell him that when I get home. No longer upset when his name is mentioned. Just enjoyment listening to our music or looking at old photographs.

But he was real and his last bottle of aftershave, which I can open and sniff, will always bring him back to me.

The Tin Box

Wages in cash every week, with a slip for deductions. At home, there was a long tin box with labelled slots in the top and separated compartments.

We sorted our money and placed an amount in each compartment: gas, electric, rates, coal, travelling costs, clothes, days out. Rest was housekeeping food etc. Everything was paid by cash. When the bills came, we would go to the office or shop to pay. There was always the unexpected bill and the need to 'borrow 'from another slot.

Later, our wages were paid into a bank – our first cheque book.

Farewell tin box!

The Photograph

I was eight years old, in Mr Smith's class, when I saw the photograph.

The war had ended three years earlier. The book was an old pre-war book, just grainy black and white pictures, I was enchanted! Mr Smith tried to explain to our young minds, the distance it covered, the people, and even said it could be seen from the moon.

Years passed, the world opened up and travel became easier but I never imagined I would see it.

Until, here I am 68 years later, standing on The Great Wall of China, staring into the distance and remembering.

The Repair Kit

I don't remember Dad teaching me to ride a bike, but I remember lots of scraped knees and elbows from falling off.

Freedom! Often off to the fields, sometimes racing each other, no helmets or pads for arms and legs, side by side or with a friend on the back. Our bikes took a lot of wear and tear on the uneven surfaces! Occasionally, a puncture!

Back home to Dad and the repair kit, bowl of water, the inner tube pumped up and placed in the bowl, looking for the telltale bubbles. Blob of glue, patch, air, and freedom again!

POLITICS & JUSTICE

What the Autumn Statement Means for You (Ian)

Are you confused by the post-pre-budget announcements by HMRC the Chancellor of the Ex-Chicory, specifically the cost-of-living upkeepdownrise as fiscalised by the Financial Oversight Undercooked Authority? Well, it's time to bust that jargon (BTJ) and get to the crux of what this means for you!

Basically, a basic base rate using base 10 of minus 2% – an inflated decrease in non-de-inflatory terms – is equal to half a legs eleven, once the retail price index finger is factored in. This equates to an un-deflated non-increase in pre-year terms following on after before.

Next week: Jargon busting ex-prime ministers. Can't wait!

One Mother. Two Motherlands (Ian)

The brothers – young and united by blood – live in a city in the east. War comes; the occupiers occupy and new borders are drawn. One brother, just outside the gates, escapes. The other, just inside the gates, remains.

The military calls and both are conscripted. Different cities. Different countries. Different armies. Different uniforms. Different aims.

They meet again, on the frontline. One, with a gun in his hand, fights for his country. One, with a gun in his back, fights for another.

Two brothers – young and united by blood… now separated by blood – lived in a city in the east.

The Detective (Ian)

A clatter of the letter box. A hurried, scribbled note: life in danger churchyard dawn

It's ten to midnight. Five hours till dawn. Time enough to solve this conundrum. I trawl the missing person's sections of the press. Phone my contacts in NYPD. Run forensics over the note. Nothing. Darn!

30 minutes till dawn. Time to catch the killer before he strikes. I head for the churchyard.

But too late. NYPD on scene. A body. I reread my note: life in danger churchyard dawn

I check the doctor's report.

Time of death: Midnight

Name: Dawn

Cause of death: Poor punctuation.

The Thin End of the Needle (Ian)

He sat waiting, sleeve rolled up. It'd been a stroke of genius, he mused, to promote an ex-GP to health secretary. She had charisma, credibility and no conscience – just the way he liked his health secretaries. This stunt to personally give him the booster live on TV was her idea; it'd do wonders for his ratings.

'Ready, Prime Minister?' she said.

'Course,' he said, giving a smile and wink to camera. 'No more than a little prick.'

She slipped the needle in.

'A little prick? You're so much more than that,' she said as, lifeless, he slumped to the floor.

The Break-in (Ian)

A knock at the door. A worried face peered through the gap. 'Yes?'

'Police, Madam. Can we come in?'

'Of course.'

'This your bedsit?'

'Yes.'

A scene of utter devastation. Wardrobe doors flung open, drawers hanging out. Clothes, sheets strewn – the carpet barely visible. A discarded jewellery box, contents scattered. Tins, packets, bottles covering every surface. Carrier bags, boxes, a suitcase... all ransacked.

The officer tutted as she tiptoed through the landmine of shoes.

'Bastards,' she muttered under her breath. 'It's the havoc they cause. What did they take?'

'Who?'

'The burglars.'

'Oh, the break-in! You need Sally next door.'

Vera (Ian)

Click clack, click clack – needles and train in perfect harmony. Until the gum-chewing youth opposite starts shouting and guffawing into his phone. He sneers, daring me to challenge him.

'Excuse me, this is the quiet carriage, would you mind…' I begin.

His guffaw is accompanied by a sneer. 'Sod off, granny!'

The other passengers shuffle uncomfortably.

'Please?'

He leans forward a middle finger leading the way, before, with a look of surprise he slumps back, silent.

I switch off his phone, wipe the blood off from the needle onto his trousers.

Click clack, click clack – needles and train in perfect harmony.

The Only Way is Ethics (Ian)

'And you'll need to appoint an Ethics Advisor.'

'Defo – never been.'

'Ethics – not Essex.'

'Why?'

'Integrity and all that. The code.'

'What code?'

'Exactly.'

'Who would they be responsible to?'

'You.'

'Well, count me in! ...Appoint that person.'

'Will do... No, they've resigned.'

'Was it something I said?'

'Yes.'

'That person?'

'Will do... they've also resigned.'

'Was it something I said?'

'Again, yes.'

'Listen, do I really need a chap at all?'

'They'll make sure everyone follows the code.'

'Even me? Hardly seems fair.'

'Are you saying having an ethics advisor is unethical?'

'Now you're talking.'

'Yes – ex-Prime Minister.'

EVERYTHING ELSE

Shoal (Ian)

When I close my eyes, I see coloured dots. They stream in from the left or right, flowing across my private world, like a shoal of fish. Tiny individual specks of life, swooping and sweeping as one. Sometimes they change direction mid-flow, but they always find a way out, up or down. I used to wonder where they went to. Now I don't.

Phosphenes, the scientists call them– electrical charges. You get them when you sneeze or stand up too quickly.

Except mine aren't phosphenes. Mine are the stars. I've seen the future and there's bad news...

They're all leaving.

Bells (Glad)

For many churches across the country, the bells calling the faithful to services or weddings or funerals is just a recording.

Emergency services bells are now pneumatic and electronic sirens.

The school bell, replaced by a buzzer, no longer rings to hasten the lazy child or to mark the end of playtime.

Now, no bells to pull outside houses, or, for the affluent, a row of bells to summon the servants.

And the rag and bone man ringing his bell is no more.

But, remember this: 'Every time a bell rings, an angel gets his wings'

IT'S A WONDERFUL LIFE!

The VAT Man Cometh (Ian)

'*And he savours another fabulous moment in a glittering career*' – I've heard several times in a sporting context, rarely outside of it.

One bleak rainy day in rundown Dalston, a businessman interrupted me as I sat on a crate in his smoky office, pouring through grubby receipts, trying to reconcile incomplete VAT records.

He stared quizzically at me before asking: 'Did you always want to be a VAT officer?'

'No.' I whispered. 'I don't know how this happened.'

The accounts never were reconciled.

Nor I to the fact that my career lacked glitter... and was completely devoid of fabulous moments.

The Cobbler (Ian)

These days he had lost track of where he was even heading. Shoes bare at the bottom, his feet hurt from walking around and around,

He had passed the shop on thousands of occasions. This time he stopped. Tentatively, he lifted the latch, a bell rang and he went in.

The cobbler was younger than he had imagined. He took off his shoes and showed him. 'They're gone,' he said grimly.

'I'll check but don't hold out much hope.'

'I won't.'

The cobbler disappeared behind the door.

He waited, staring dully at the sign which read:

LOST SOLES

Tri-ians (Ian)

Two smart gentlemen walked up my drive, here to tell me all about God. I could tell. I don't usually open the door, but if I do, I always promptly, politely send them on their way. Today, I hesitated.

'Hello!' one of them said with a hopeful smile. 'My name's Ian. And this,' he continued, 'is also Ian.'

Two Ians on my doorstep. A coincidence? An act of God? Maybe. Except, my name's Ian, too! Three Ians. A connection! An Eph-ian–y?

My heart said: 'Tell them your name! It'll make their day!'

My mouth said: 'Sorry... I'm a Catholic.'

The Horse That Doesn't Rock (Ian)

In my attic, tucked away under a dusty cloth, is my old rocking horse. Brought into this world by a Victorian, she's a long way past her best.

Her dazzling trappings are fading away, the once flowing white mane is straggly and grey, her markings haggard and worn. Abandoned and lacking sunlight, she's no longer saddled with great expectations – the Miss Havisham of the equestrian world. Yet there's hope, for she shares my dark attic with others, discarded and unloved – my collection of 70s LPs.

And just like Showwaddywaddy and Elvis, the horse that doesn't rock, might well rock again

The Silhouette (Ian)

The boy watched the silhouette approach, growing in size and menace. Behind it, the evening sunlight skipped across the lake, tiny explosions of glitter. It was stunning; a stark contrast to the horror that was about to unfold.

The slaves had carried their masters' cargo for weeks, along animal tracks, across rivers, up steep mountains. But the food had run out and their captors were hungry. The silhouette would decide who would be their next meal.

They huddled together while the boy covered his face with his arm.

He heard sighs of relief all around him.

The silhouette had chosen.

Tunnel Vision (Ian)

To be part of the gang he had to prove himself. And he needed to be part of the gang. In the tough streets, there was no light at the end of the tunnel, only survival.

'It's not far,' the leader said. 'Exit point there. Do it.'

The boy hesitated, then seeing the sneering look of the others, sunk to his knees, pushed his head and shoulders into the hole and scrabbled downwards into the blackness.

As he crawled further in, cold penetrating his bones, he realised, with dread, there was no light at the end of this tunnel either.

We're Here for You (Ian)

'Morning. How can we help?'

'I have a problem.'

'Oh, dear. Who would you like to assist you today? Us up here, or our colleagues below?'

'What's the difference?'

'It's mainly skillsets. Our angels are good with the softer ones – counselling, that sort of thing. Demons are more no-nonsense. Tell it straight. And they're good at putting up shelves.'

'Shelves?'

'Yes. Tell me about your problem.'

'I'm a bit lost.'

'Okay: path of righteousness is us. Being led astray, them.'

'The help I need is more specific.'

'How?'

'I'm in Colchester, looking for Debenhams.'

'Debenhams? Sorry, we don't do miracles.'

Paul's Revolutionary Object-maker (Ian)

The contestants for '*Surviving on a Desert Island with Just One Object*' revealed the one object they would take.

'My object's a knife.'

'Mine's a tent.'

'A water filter.'

And so it continued until it was Smug Paul from Colchester's turn.

'I've invented my own revolutionary object-maker. Feed in any raw materials, type what object you want and it spews it out. I can have anything!'

Later, on Paul's desert island, the audience watched him set it up. Audience ratings peaked at 30 million watching Paul spend his remaining time on the island, hunting for somewhere to plug it in.

Pithiness Personified (Ian)

Accused of being verbose, I've decided to cut the crap, strip everything down to the bare bones, and waste not one word on pointless, ineffective, unnecessary, inconsequential adjectives, adverbs, nouns, verbs, pronouns, prepositions, conjunctions and interjections that add virtually, or barely, nothing, nil, zilch, diddly-squat to what I say.

'Brevity' is my watchword, my slogan, my mantra. It'll be embedded in my soul, my core, my philosophy. Henceforth, in the future, from this day onwards, there'll be no more elaborating, padding out, blah-de-blah or yak-yakking.

Concise and to the point.

No one can take the pith out of me now.

Story Inspiration (Ian)

Story writing is tricky. I look for inspiration around me, like the photo I took of a swan staring at its reflection in the water. There's a story, I thought.

I jotted down random questions to help build a plot.

Had it been told to get out of town recently?

What did it do all through the wintertime?

Was it ashamed to show its face in fear of what others might say?

What happened to the stubby brown feathers?

If you have a photo, maybe 3 bears eating porridge or a wolf blowing down houses, try my method. It works!

THANKS TO...

This book has been put together for you, the reader, and for my mum, Gladys, hoping that she will enjoy seeing in print the stories we have written.

During Lockdown, Mum walked around her house to stay fit, encouraging family and friends around her to do similar by writing hilarious (and sometimes poignant) emails in which she would pretend that she was walking around dressed up as different famous people. (See story page 57).

After I got involved in writing 100-word stories, she decided to have a go, too, to pass away Lockdown time. If you've read the stories, you may have noticed that many of hers are based on true things that have happened, providing snapshots of her life. They are the ying to the mainly frivolous yang of mine. I hope you have enjoyed them.

*So, **thanks to my mum**, for being an inspiration to us generally, and to me, specifically, for inspiring me to write.*

*Very big thanks also has to go to the following people involved in **Bill's Big Bag of Onions** – the catalyst for our stories.*

***Bill Lawrance** who is the Bill in the show and the host. Bill also writes stories for the show.*

***Adrian Cohen,** the producer, director, voice artist, and story contributor. The driving force behind the show.*

***Yvonne Pini,** another excellent voice artist, and also a story contributor.*

***Toni Baxter Peers** who introduced me to the show. She also writes 100-word stories.*

*And, finally, thanks to our fellow **Onioners** whose stories make for fantastic entertainment.*

To hear these stories and others brought to life in audio form, listen to **Bill's Big Bag of Onions** on **Colne Radio** on **106.6 FM** and on Spotify.

ABOUT THE AUTHOR

Ian And Gladys Hornett

Ian is an author of cozy mysteries and sci-fi books, and Gladys is the mother of an author of cozy mysteries and sci-fi books.

She takes all gentle ribbing by Ian in good heart and humour... thankfully.

BOOKS BY THIS AUTHOR

Maggie Matheson: The Senior Spy

81-year-old Maggie has everything: a warm flat, fresh sea air, good friends, and someone who comes to cut her toenails once a month. But when a mysterious young man contacts her after a near-death encounter with a pizza peel, her cosy, comfortable life is set to become decidedly less cosy and considerably more uncomfortable... which is just as well, since Maggie is bored stiff.

Meet Maggie Matheson: octogenarian, tea lover, bridge enthusiast, and kick-ass spy.

Maggie Matheson: Down Undercover

Waking up on top of Sydney Harbour Bridge tied to her great-grandson is not the fun family reunion Maggie had planned. Sinister and powerful forces are at work. Operating off-grid, Maggie will have to rely on the old ways – and an old friend – if she is going to crack this case.

Tapped into the Dreamtime world of a local indigenous tribe and tapped out of anything remotely I.T. related, she is in her element.

Tank-driver, master of disguise, and international spy, Maggie Matheson, is back – Down Undercover.

Maggie Matheson: Last Orders

Bruised and battered after her last case, Maggie is a shadow of her feisty former self. But when a double-dealing double agent threatens to disclose nuclear codes, she is inclined to answer her country's call to help. The opportunity to heal past hurts seals the deal.

Meanwhile, other shady individuals are at large; shady individuals who want to make sure she goes out with a whimper and a bang. Does she still have the cunning, courage and clout to crack the case? Will her last orders be a curtain call? Or is it finally curtains for Maggie?

Last Orders is the third and final cosy mystery book in the Maggie Matheson Collection. Essential feel-good reading for fans of Richard Osman's Murder Club

Quarton: The Bridge

Surviving in a city devastated by a nuclear attack,

Fen has had to be resourceful, resilient and ready for anything. The discovery of the quarton block – the one remaining stone created to power a bridge between two worlds – lures her in and throws her already dangerous life as a scavenger into turmoil. Fen suddenly finds herself traveling a path that was set for her in a previous life on an alien planet, thousands of years ago.

But there are others who have been pulled into the quarton's domain. Like Fen, they have lived many times before. And they exist for one purpose: to claim the last quarton.

What started as a battle for personal survival has become a battle to decide the future of two worlds.

Quarton: The Coding

After 7,000 years, the last quarton has been destroyed and so too have the hopes of the great schemer, Arrix, to rebuild the Garial Bridge to Earth. 7,000 years spent searching for the quarton blocks, living and dying over and over again, have been wasted. But the coding within the quartons is powerful and resilient, qualities its keepers must have in abundance if they are to live forever. When a vast hole appears in the sky over England, the alien phenomenon proves to be beyond the comprehension of everyone on the planet. Everyone except a bad-tempered scientist with a score to settle, his gentle giant assistant, and the one person on the other side of the world who wants nothing whatsoever to do with it.

She is determined she will build a new life that does not involve powerful stones, bridges or aliens.
The coding - and Arrix - are equally determined she won't.

Quarton: The Payback

Trapped light years from Earth, Fen faces a perilous journey through alien terrain to return to the planet where Arrix and Klavon have joined forces to wreak havoc. Desperation to be with her daughter forces her on. But underneath, anger and vengeance seethe – and the coding thrives. With the coding, Fen will be like Arrix and Klavon. Without the coding, she can't get home. The scene is set for one final encounter between the four Garalians who were on the original bridge. Whoever can control the coding, can control the future. The quartons and the coding have not quite finished wielding their influence just yet.

Quarton: The Payback - the final installment in the mind-bending Quarton Series.

The Lockdown, The Walks And The Wardrobe By Gladys Hornett

The hilarious recount of an 80 year old granny trying to stay fit and active during lockdown in the UK in 2020, told through light-hearted emails to friends and family.

Printed in Great Britain
by Amazon

38998669R00076